The Call of Samay

A short story

IBA PANDA

ISBN: 978-93-5426-474-0

DEDICATION

This book is dedicated to my loving parents and dear husband, who have always inspired me to dream big and follow my heart.

"It is better to conquer yourself than to win a thousand battles. Then the victory is yours. It cannot be taken from you."

~Buddha

CONTENTS

ACKNOWLEDGMENTS

Writing is a path usually treaded upon alone. This is what people say. But if I speak from my experience, then it's a lie. I have been supported by a group of dedicated people, who have worked hard to make my first book into a reality. Anshuman, my husband, who has advised me through all the aspects of this book and has been the inspiration behind the completion of this book. Ritu Poddar, for editing this book. She made my elementary English far better and made the flow of the story so much more refined. Ansuman Nayak for his advice and support for digital marketing and promotions. Ankita Mohapatra, my cousin, who believed that this book is worth publishing. Last but not the least, you! the reader who has given me your most valuable possession, your time.

PREFACE

The year 2020 has been one of the most challenging years in human history. An invisible virus has changed the way in which human beings' function. Along with the changes in our external environment, there has been a sea of change in the internal system of people. Human beings all around the world are in an emotional vortex, and this book is an attempt towards inner introspection. The value of introspection has been ingrained in the cultural heritage of Bharata i.e., India. Bharata has always been a land of seekers. Seekers who seek the purpose of their existence, and who have managed to attain inner peace despite the hostile environment around them. In these difficult times, this story tries to delve deep into the inner thoughts of human beings in order to find solace, which is the need of the hour. This work is a tribute to one of the greatest seekers of this land, Siddhartha! and to the lessons that he has bestowed upon us. Within those lessons is the lesson that bliss and misery happen within and not outside.

PROLOGUE

Heavy, torrential rain was pouring down. Amidst the cold, windy weather, I could sense the exasperation of mother nature towards humanity. The grey, persistent clouds had spread across the vast sky that had made the environment dark and shady. Within the darkness, the sun battled with the clouds to spread its golden rays.

The gloomy weather glided me into a pensive mood and many abstract thoughts started crossing my mind. Where is the end to the vagaries of life? Can this world ever enjoy the essence of peace? Why there is this never-ending desire for Karmic fruit? Why is there so much of hatred and chaos all around? The present societal condition was hurting me from within. Amidst the inner turmoil, I dozed off.

Against the dimming sky, my sleepy eyes caught sight of a faint silhouette approaching towards me. In the darkness, I couldn't get a clear view of the face. But could only see a hand holding a small lit lamp. Startled I asked," Who?" I'm Samay, came an answer, I've been existing since the beginning of the universe and will continue even after. I am eternal!

I'm here to take you with me to find answers to the questions that have been creating turbulence in your mind.

The inner thirst of knowing all answers to the sprouting questions made me follow Samay's footsteps. Uninterrupted rain kept gushing down while the thunder roared through the sky. But we walked through all that, undeterred!

At last, we reached a riverbank and sat on a boat. It seemed as if the boat was waiting for us. I asked Samay, where are you taking me now? Without saying anything, Samay only pointed towards the wide silvery river. That vast ocean-like river appeared like my limitless thoughts. Dancing with the ripples of water our boat kept sailing forward.

Couldn't estimate how many banks and for how long our boat had sailed across. It felt like we were heading towards a memorable destination of history by crossing river after river under the massive galaxy. During this long journey, I had gone into a deep slumber. Don't know for how long! Suddenly, I woke up to find myself on an extensive riverbank, with the boat anchored to the shore, and Samay asking me to accompany him.

This page has been intentionally left blank

HOW I CAME ACROSS SIDDHARTHA…

Far away on the river bank, our eyes fell on a simple, calm and composed village girl. But her face revealed unhappiness and tiredness. Tears rolled down her cheeks and eventually flowed into the depths of the river. She stood up from the bank and started walking down towards her home through the dense forest at her own pace. After sometime, again, that girl came out of her house and started walking down a narrow lane. She was holding a plate on her two open palms. It had some food in it, and the docile faced girl kept walking briskly.

Samay overtook her and blocked her path. He asked- Can I know your name, please? Momentarily the girl stood still, staring at his face. After a second, she answered, my name is Sujata.

The name was beautiful meaning how auspicious her birth is. Sujata! Her feet were becoming impatient to restart the journey, but Samay was still standing in front of her. His questions had not yet finished.

Where are you going? For whom is this food kept on this plate? The eyes of Sujata got filled with tears.

She started saying, move from my path, let me go.

Within an instant, his life will be gone. He has not eaten for days now. I have been watching him in this forest for the last six years.

How beautiful and mesmerising his face and form is. But do you know what that young man used to do?

For days and days, he kept torturing himself, and now he is lying in front of death. In the scorching heat of summer, he would be sitting on the burning rocks, watching the radiant face of the sun for hours together.

Similarly, in freezing winter, he would submerge himself in the ice-cold water of this river. He would be standing rock-steady beneath heavy downpour in rainy days for hours and hours.

Sometimes my eyes would see him sitting somewhere near torrid forest fire or on a bed of thorns, lost in his own world! He would gladly embrace all the stings of poisonous insects and attacks of any dangerous wild beast. For days after days, he stood on his one leg. His eyes could not sleep for so many nights altogether.

How could one be so cruel towards his body!

Over many years I have been watching his strange activities, without him knowing.

Again, he has started complete fasting. He is barely holding onto his life by abandoning all his thirst and hunger. But, for how long will this be possible! There is just a skeleton left with mere skin wrapped over it, eyes sunk into the sockets.

Now, no energy is left in his body to even get up. His existence is about to end. So, kindly clear my path and let me rush.

I'm taking only this much food for him. Will throw myself under his feet. If he looks at, will plead before him- hail you! Extraordinary human, you deep meditator, please accept food from my hands and help yourself to stay alive.

Samay then stepped aside, clearing her route. Sujata quietly walked past into the thick green woods.

Some time flew by. Suddenly, a very heartbreaking scene caught our eyes as we were heading on our path into the jungle. Little distance away, we saw an external framework of bones, covered with a thin layer of skin, seated on a mud pavilion, completely steady, still and stagnant. It was impossible to find out whether the bodily like structure was alive or dead. In the meantime, Sujata threw herself at the feet of this surreal figurine. She had surrendered her whole being in front of him.

Unstoppable tears started rolling down from her eyes. She was murmuring something in a thin, shrill voice. We then realised that life force had started flowing through the skeletal body. Eyes had begun to open slowly from the sockets. It seemed as if the open eyes were showering blessings on Sujata.

Sujata raised her arms, offering the food plate. Gradually, the lean and thin hands of the human-like sculpture came down. Those hands picked up a very little quantity of food and took it towards the mouth. This made Sujata's life worthy and fulfilling. She was able to save a human's life from the verge of death.

I asked Samay- Who is this person? Why is he carrying such an uncommon form?

Before I could get an answer from Samay, I saw that the pale young man was rising up. With great difficulty and by gathering all his energies together, he has now stood up. He started moving step by step towards the bank of river "Niranjana". After refreshing himself in the river water, he came back up to the shore. At a constant pace, he kept his steps one by one towards a large banyan tree. The tree stood erect right in the middle of thick heavy woods. The highest branches of the banyan tree spread in all directions. It formed a dense canopy along with its varied roots hanging down towards the mud ground.

This skeleton-like man sat under the massive shade with his eyes closed. In the middle of all these instances, Sujata had already left. Samay took me a little distance away by holding my hand. The nature around me indeed was splendid and breath-taking. Under the free sunlit sky stood the majestic, glorious forest, "Uruvela". Its shade and freshness spread in all the four directions.

Again, I asked Samay- Who is this man? Why is he holding such an unusual form? Why in this dangerous dense jungle is he sitting all alone?

Samay was also looking too serious as if he was about to go into the stage of rumination! But he replied- The name of this person is Siddhartha.

WHO IS SIDDHARTHA?

Once upon a time, he was a prince of Kapilavastu kingdom. A loving son of king Shuddhodhana, with endless property and wealth, heavenly abode, celestial provisions and enjoyment, amazingly beautiful wife Yashodhara, newborn baby boy Rahul — he has left behind everything. The inner quest to seek the truth of his very existence in this world filled with untruth is the only reason for the condition that he is going through. He is wandering in search of an answer which he has not found yet.

But what is the question? I asked.

What is life? What is the meaning of this world? Why there is birth? Why there is death? From where is this soul coming? To where is this soul going back? Why is it coming into this world? Why there is so much pain? Why there is misery? What is the ultimate result of this life? The prince's heart is full and burdened with these kinds of unending questions. He has been going through so much of turmoil, hard assiduousness in search of his question's answers.

And now this strong promise to himself. Until his soul is not satisfied with the answers he is in search of, he will undergo deep penance and meditation. From this deep meditation, he will achieve enlightenment.

Samay had been speaking continuously. In his description, he even detailed the past life of the prince.

The ancient kingdom of Kapilavastu that lies at the foothills of the Himalayas, spreads between the country of Kosala on the west and Koliyas on the east. It was a stable kingdom that flourished during the time of King Suddhodhana, father of Prince Siddhartha Gautama. In this city, Prince spent his early years after his birth until he left the palace at the age of 29. Kapilavastu is considered the childhood home of the Prince on account of it being the capital of the Shakyas, over whom his father ruled.

BIRTH OF THE PRINCE

King Shuddhodhana had a queen named Mayadevi. After a few years of marriage, the queen was expecting with a baby. In her tenth month, she decided to go to her father's place, Lumbini.

While she was on her way and the chariot was about to reach Lumbini, her eyes fell on an alluring grove. She got attracted by its aura and wanted to spend some time there. So, she ordered the charioteer, "stop the chariot." Slowly she stepped down and started walking towards the serene ambience. While enjoying the peaceful scenery, she started experiencing labour pain. Then in that soothing, calm environment on a full moon night of Baisakh, the Prince was born to her.

When the king heard this news, his joy had no bounds. In his state of ecstasy, he immediately rushed to bring back his queen and son to Kapilavastu. After the return of the king, sage Asita visited the palace to see their newborn baby. As soon as he saw the baby, his eyes were filled with tears.

On seeing Sage's such reaction, the King very curiously asked him the reason behind his unhappiness. The sage in a poignant manner answered," the boy in future will either become a King of Kings…or a great saint. But alas, I wouldn't be alive to witness this and listen to his great words."

Hearing Sage's words, both king and queen were happy. On the fifth day, the baby was named "Siddhartha Gautama". Then the king decided that he would work towards making his son a great emperor and not a saint.

THE EARLY LIFE

As Siddhartha was growing up, it became evident that he was born for bigger things. He was not only handsome, brave and fearless but also kind and soft-hearted. He loved to spend his time alone, under a "Jambu" tree, and this made the king anxious about the prophecy.

Once, while walking in the palace gardens, Siddhartha saw a bird fall down after being hit by an arrow. He immediately rushed towards the bird and removed it from its body. Siddhartha felt as if the arrow had pierced his own heart. As he sat there, nursing the bird, his cousin Devadutta arrived and demanded that the bird be handed over to him, as he had shot the bird. This bird is so beautiful, why do you want to hurt it? Siddhartha asked. However, Devadutta was adamant. The matter was then taken to the court.

There the king asked the prince, What right do you have to keep the bird? Then Siddharth explained that if he had not removed the arrow, the bird would have died, "After saving, the bird now owes its life to me. Should the bird belong to the one who tried to take its life or to the one who gave back its life?", said Siddhartha.

Hearing the interpretation, one of the Noble judges present in the court answered that whatever the prince said was correct. The one who saved the life of the bird has a greater right. Finally, he gave the judgement saying, "Devadutta, the bird belongs to the prince."

Many years passed on. One day, the Swayamvara of princess Yashodhara was being held. Princes from far and near including prince Siddhartha came to attend the Swayamvara. Amidst the gathering, eyes of the princess fell on the handsome prince Siddhartha. She immediately felt that he is the one whom she wants to spend her life with, and prayed for his triumph in the competition to be held.

The entire universe as if conspired to make her wishes come true. The prince attained victory in all the tests, be it horse-riding, archery or swordsmanship. After the grand success, Siddhartha and Yashodhara were married with great pomp and show.

Soon after marriage, a son named "Rahul" was born to them. King Suddhodhana was extremely pleased to hear the news and thought to himself that his son Siddhartha from then onwards would never think of becoming a saint.

After becoming a father, the prince wanted to go out of the palace and explore more of the outer world. He then asked permission from his father to which the king responded that he would like to

order a special chariot for him so that he can go out sitting on it comfortably. Even the king made sure that during the tour of the city, all sights of unhappiness, misery, sorrow, should be kept away from Siddhartha.

But the Almighty always has his own plans. His heavenly plans are far beyond the earthly sense.

TOWARDS THE PATH OF RENUNCIATION

On his first day of the tour in Kapilavastu, something happened like this. Young beautiful prince, Siddhartha sat on his chariot. The charioteer was sitting in front of him, and the chariot kept moving fast on its path. An unknown person was walking very slowly beside the garden. When the prince's eyes fell on that stranger, he gave orders to stop the chariot. His eyes kept on staring at that helpless person. He was very old, his body was suffering from illness. His skin was dry and rough with grey hair on his head. There were no teeth in his mouth with negligible eyesight in his eyes. His legs didn't even have enough strength to hold his own body weight. His hands were holding a stick which provided support to his weak body. There was no energy, no strength and no capability left. One after another he kept his footsteps with much agony and pain. In a way of saying, nothing fresh and crisp was left in the pale body of that old man except for his life—the weight of which he had been carrying and will carry till his death.

Seeing this sight, the prince's mind got full of strange thoughts. He asked the charioteer, why is the person like this?

Charioteer answered, hail Lord! This is the stage of old age. Any person who is alive in this world someday or the other will witness this phase of life. Old age is the precursor to the end of life.

The vulnerable prince ordered, take back the chariot. His longing to enjoy the lush green garden's beauty had almost died. The painful observation of old age had already created a storm of curiosity in the mind and heart of the young prince, Siddhartha.

One by one questions had already started knocking his brain cells.

Where will this young, energetic, full life body go? What will happen to this body at an old remote age?

Chariot had already taken the reverse path. Siddhartha was sitting with a very serious face, lost in his deep thoughts. Charioteer observed his disturbed state of mind. His beautiful face had disappeared into the shadows of contemplation. At the same time, the upper limbs of the sun were disappearing below the horizon.

An incident of another day. That day again the prince was travelling to the other end of the kingdom in his chariot. Far away a beautifully decorated room was visible. Shining with the intense orange and red colour of twilight. Soothing melodious music was audible to the ears as the chariot was nearing the room. But suddenly, a man's agonising aching voice was heard from nowhere. The throbbing cries made the prince's eyes roll around in search of the voice. Finally, his eyes fell upon a person sitting on the roadside.

Immediately prince gave orders to the charioteer to stop the chariot. He then kept staring at the unknown man to find out what was wrong with him. The man's body was full of abnormal spots as if he was suffering from some illness.

The body was already in a rotten stage. Various parts had disintegrated and were about to decompose. But still, there was life in the body. Helplessly, he was lying on the roadside gazing into the infinite space. Because of the unbearable torment and pain, very faint, feeble and broken sounds kept coming out of his mouth. Prince just kept staring at him. The state of affair continued, and myriads of moments elapsed.

Then prince Siddhartha asked the charioteer — Why is this man in such a peculiar condition?

The charioteer answered —hail Lord! The man has been attacked by a dreadful disease and he has no strength to fight it. Each and every second his body is struggling unbearable pain, agony and suffering to keep hold of that uncertain life within. There's no other way out. Ailments and diseases are part and parcel of life. They can attack a human's body anytime, anywhere without one's awareness. If there is life, sickness is sure to come. In front of illness, every body, is equal. It creates no discrimination between the King and his subjects, rich and poor, young and old. Maladies are always lurking like shadows from birth until death in a human's life.

Whosoever is born on this earth can never ever escape from pain and misery. This is the ultimate truth of human's life.

Siddhartha kept staring at that ailing person for quite a long time. His eyes were filled with tear droplets. He was completely still and perplexed. At last, he said— "take back the chariot." If for this body such kind of diseases and pain has been created, then what is the meaning of all these enjoyment and amusement. The chariot returned. The sight of that unlucky person suffering from dreadful disease got etched in Siddhartha's mind. What is the meaning of this pale body? What is its value? He kept pondering about all these questions the whole night. But couldn't get any answers. But he got to realise that the mortal body is nothing but a mere paradox, on this earth.

Now, on another afternoon. Seated on his chariot, Siddhartha was crossing the path of the decorated, joyful city. The chariot was being followed by a platoon of soldiers, along with some pedestrians who were struggling, just to get a glance of their loving prince.

The delightful crowd kept singing songs of praises, showering flowers on him and praying for the long-life of the king and the prince.

On the opposite side of Rajpath, a small procession was visible. Men and women walking in the procession left the Rajpath for the prince's chariot, that was approaching from the other side and took a narrow path instead. Even though they saw the prince's chariot was coming all the way, the mass did not stop and just kept walking. Siddhartha's eyes fell on that unusual cavalcade. Everybody kept mourning continuously. He saw a covered human body being carried on their shoulders. Only the face was visible. Varieties of flowers adorned the body. But there was no end to the mourning and anguish of the people, carrying the body.

Charioteer! What am I seeing? The prince asked in a very disturbed manner. The charioteer replied, Hey! King's son; this is a man's dead body. They are taking their dear one's dead body for cremation. His breath has stopped. Within a span of time, this dead body will turn into ashes. The ashes will eventually get diluted in the soil. Death is the ultimate end of life. Whatever may be the circumstances, in this vast world no-one can be saved from death. This flesh and bone body one day will turn into the soil of this mother earth.

Siddhartha kept staring at the body, absolutely shocked by the charioteer's words. His eyes were exploding with emotions completely captivated by the eternally closed eyes of the dead body. How subtle the face of the dead body appeared. Where has the shine of life disappeared! Where is the liveliness! Where is the grace of name, fame, pride and dignity!

Within that moment Siddhartha had told many unclear things to himself. If death is the only truth, then why so much pain, struggle, anxiety for life? For this life and body, there is fathomless greed. Endless desires to be fulfilled. In the ocean of desires and dreams, so many actions performed, unending aspirations and struggles! What is the significance of all these? Meanwhile, the procession of the dead body had passed away. But the chariot of the prince was standing still. The crowd following their prince was also standing still. He told the charioteer to take back the chariot. In the middle of his joyful city tour, he got to see an image of death— the first activity seemed a lie to him; the second one is the ultimate truth he came to know.

Within the limitless time he could see the endless death procession of humans. Neither there is end of wayfarer nor end to this great journey. With the numbers amounting to millions and billions; century after century, from the beginning of the universe, this journey is going on. The mourning ceremonies of innumerable dead bodies! This is what is life, thinks Siddhartha Gautama.

Some days have passed by. One day in the middle of an afternoon, Siddhartha was returning from an unknown place by riding his horse. The "Rajpath" seemed deserted due to the scorching heat. A lone person was walking down the empty path. Siddhartha's eyes fell on this lonely man. He was holding a very calm, patient and poised personality. Only a simple loincloth was covering his body.

The mid-afternoon sun-rays were falling directly on his face. Still, there was no sign of frown. Complete peace and calmness just blossomed from his face. No tension, no grief, no pain. Absolute fearless the traveller was. He had no affection for life nor any attraction towards the world. He seemed to have abandoned his near and dear ones, mother, father, brother, sister, everybody. He had freed himself from the hands of fallacy and fantasy of the world. No place, no shelter, no family, no friends, nothing he had. In that futility also he was the happiest. Because those who have everything, they constantly keep thinking and worrying only about the things that they have. Neither there is an end to it nor any way to escape from it.

Siddhartha realised, that person must be a “sannyasi”. That “sannyasi” just vanished within a second. But his calm and poised stature was already etched in the prince’s mind. His eminence was in-erasable, his aura was extremely joyful.

There was no end to Siddhartha’s thoughts. He kept thinking—Isn't renunciation the real path of peace? Wasn't the “sannyasi” a highly intellectual man, who has abandoned all the desires and expectations from the presumed notion of the world held by people? He chose this path amongst this ignorance and darkness, to get the real light of spirituality as he thought that to be the best. By now, Siddhartha’s thoughts had increased a million times from before.

THE JOURNEY BEGINS…

Father Suddhodhana started pondering seeing his son's change of mind and heart. He tried many things to sway his beloved son's mind from all these troubling thoughts.

Grand palace started echoing with the sounds of ankle bells worn around the feet of alluring dancers. Sweet music around the corners of the palace lighted everybody's heart and soul. Various types of merry-making and frolicking activities were being carried out in the palace for entertainment and pleasure of the king's son. Everywhere there were just waves of happiness and jolliness. A warm welcome to all kinds of luxury and grandeur. Everyone's heart was filled with joy and satisfaction. But the person for whom all these arrangements were made, he himself was filled with discontentment. Siddhartha's dissatisfied unhappy heart was heavy with unprecedented thoughts. Questions after questions. But no answers!

Tension and anxiety had now become the only all-time associate of king's son. Temptation after temptation, the attraction of fondness, allurement of this materialistic world, everything seemed to have failed in front of Prince

Siddhartha. Inner pain and agony were the only successful outcome that kept on increasing with time. But the pain he felt was not his own. He was hurt again and again by the sufferings and torment of mankind. This melancholy weighed heavily in his heart.

At last, in the womb of infinite time came an auspicious night. In the middle of the dark night, king's son Siddhartha Gautama came out of the Kapilavastu palace. In front of him lay an endless journey to cover. He was a lone pilgrim in an unknown unpredictable path in search of life's truth.

THE ENLIGHTENED ONE!

“Samay” had been telling many such things. But I was unable to hear anymore. Because my mind was completely occupied by the unusual story of the king’s son Siddhartha. By the time I came back to the present moment, I saw Siddhartha standing up from his deep penance and meditation under the big banyan tree. His face was radiating like a bright sun. He could feel eternal contentment and happiness.

Samay told—in his meditation he has found answers to his questions. With the help of this wisdom that he has achieved, from now onwards he will be called as “Buddha”. From this moment, for the sake of this mankind, he will be an epitome of eternal truth and ultimate wisdom. His wisdom and knowledge will spread worldwide. The ancient "Banyan Tree" and "Uruvela" became blessed forever. And the river "Niranjana" remained venerable for generations to come.

At that time Buddha had already walked away from the cool shadow of the “Bodhi” tree. He was just marching ahead into the dense forest of “Uruvela”. His journey continued with immense motivation and enlightenment. Such extraordinary energy came out from that slender and svelte body. That's why he is Buddha! He is powerful by his wisdom. Enlightened by life's truth.

We kept following him. Crossing far off roads surrounded by dangerous forest, lakes, rivers etc. we kept moving ahead with indomitable hope of getting to hear his words of wisdom. Our mind kept wondering — What is his discovered truth! What is the value of this truth! that he will be expressing at his own decided place?

From far off, our eyes caught hold of a vibrant new place in the lap of nature. Varanasi city, along the banks of the river Ganga, was a few miles away. A cool breeze was flowing around the green and beautiful scenery. Ferns and petals, green fresh climbers and trees just increased the glory of the place.

The environment was entirely calm and peaceful, with not a single person around. The name of the place is Sarnath.

There we saw, that Buddha sat on a high raised mud pavilion, which was covered by a vast canopy of dense green trees. Five persons were sitting near his feet. They will first listen to Buddha's enchanting words. They kept staring at his face. Completely hypnotised and mesmerised with his divine personality. There was this shine of absolute tranquility on his face.

He slowly started his speech of truth and harmony— This world is a lie. It is temporary, this human life incoherent. Materialism is meaningless. It's momentary. But alas this world! Alas, human's worldly life! The shadow of misery and sorrow has crept over everywhere. Mankind is full of agony. Intolerable is the pain, that fills life with wretchedness. Immense tension, torment and suffering are the main causes of unhappiness. Oh, man! find the solution to protect yourself from the infinite depth of misery. Try to identify the real cause of pain and sorrow. This birth is painful, suffering is painful, illness is painful. Within the life lies hopelessness, disappointment and non-fulfilment.

Thus, anguish and affliction fill the entire existence. So, try to think of the ways to eradicate unhappiness.

With his teachings, Buddha tried to comfort. The main reason for distress is desire. Human's desires are limitless. They keep increasing and spreading in a various number of ways. Life continues to struggle within that fire of endless desires and hopes. But again, life continues just by holding onto the same yearning. A man's quest is too deep and vast with never-ending wishes and fancies.

If life is just a momentary dream, then what is the meaning of holding onto this worldliness! This world is nothing but a profess of lies. Within this bewilderment, man is in search of false happiness. To fulfil some wishful thoughts, man undergoes so many good and bad deeds. He is always in quest of so many ways and methods to achieve his wants both physically and mentally. To fulfil his wants and desires, he suffers the consequences of his actions for so many lives. Birth happens only for these unfulfilled desires. And with the onset of life, unhappiness creeps in.

Yes, it's true, that with extreme desperation, a human is continuously running after eternal felicity. But in actual, what is he getting? Only sadness and dejection. It's because life's real happiness doesn't lie in the material luxuries of this world. Even though one does get it, it's just a lie—momentary happiness.

So oh, you human! Death of desire is the death of distress. A desire-less human's contentment is immeasurable. He experiences the real ecstasy. Nothing is comparable to this divine bliss, neither any worldly lust nor hunger nor thirst. For him, nothing else matters. Not even life nor death. He has already become one with soul, attaining an exuberant high spirit.

Therefore oh, human! If you are holding onto this life, then take this life to such a level where you can easily breakthrough from all kinds of worldly desires and aspirations. Practising liberation from all desires should be the ultimate pledge of life. Ways to break all the ties and free oneself from all the worldly things lie here itself.

Yes, it is true that the cycle of "Karma" is rolling on. The imprisoned life of humans is continuously getting crushed beneath its wheels. During the entire existence, the cursed soul cries in great pain beneath the burden of "Karma". There is no end to it even after death because the cycle of rebirth continues. Rebirth is again no different from this birth, as the same seeds of desire germinate. It then leads to the same sorrow and misery. The want, to fulfil infinite longings and aspirations leads to the origin of work. And this work gives birth to the hope for the final result. To enjoy this result, the cycle of birth continues. Life after death, death after life, the cycle continues to spin its wheels. Help yourself to make your soul free from this deep eternal cycle. For this, there are various ways. Paths are lying open in front of you. Start your journey on these new paths.

The name of this new path is the "Eightfold path". This path consists of eight practices: right view, right resolve, right speech, right conduct, right livelihood, right effort, right mindfulness and right samadhi. By practising this noble "Eightfold path", experience your pure soul, make your life disciplined, keep your thoughts clear and unadulterated, attain absolute bliss and finally discover the ultimate truth of life.

For a moment, Buddha closed his eyes! The disciples started blooming with pleasure with this new ray of hope. The light of truth is now shining from within. They came to realise that the noble path is not that difficult. Any normal human being can easily accept this path to get rid of the vicious cycle of birth and rebirth.

Buddha opened his eyes! His eyes reflected compassion and mercy. He started preaching his disciples— Even the vast oceans are minuscule before the painful tears of man. His earthly happiness is just an alias of the vicious cycle of poisonous results. The selfish human needs a divine vision to realise the peace, that lies beyond selfishness. By crossing the boundaries, of the results of “Karma”, and overcoming his longings and aspirations, man can make himself free from this continuous cycle.
Then only the free soul will move towards the attainment of “Nirvana”.

All the disciples bowed down with utmost respect. I looked towards Samay. At that moment he was also in the deep mode of imploring, with his eyes closed and hands joined together. In front of Buddha's auspicious form, he had also converted himself into one of his disciples. I immediately closed my eyes.

After a few moments Samay said— From this instance, Buddha will start his journey. His journey of travelling around the world would last for almost 45 years. His pious feet will touch each and every corner, from the foothills of Himalayas to the vast Gangetic plains. Disciples will increase in huge numbers and will spread all around the world. This holy place "Bharata" will start shining with the light of new hope and ambition.

Peace, friendship, love, non-violence and humanity will spread like large waves in every corner of this sphere. The thought of equality will germinate in each human's heart and mind. There would be no difference between a king and his subjects, rich and poor, the Brahmins and the Shudras, and between various colours and creeds. Uncountable humans will fall at his feet with the utmost respect to experience his divine teachings.

But Buddha will be walking away on his own path with "Nirmanakaya" physical form, holding a small alms-bowl in his hand. Wholly lost in his sermons. His teachings of "Noble" paths of how to lead this life, will be touching the hearts of millions.

With extreme fascination, I kept on listening to Samay. Suddenly from the forest of Sarnath, a melodious song of the disciples came floating towards us—

Buddham, Sharanam, Gacchami...

We then started returning towards the boat. On the way, I asked — Samay, did Buddha's sanctimonious teachings really take the human race, onto a righteous path?

Samay remained silent for a long time. Maybe he was not in a mood to answer my question. But finally, with great reluctance, Samay answered - Yes it's true that gradually Buddha's teachings spread like a religion in the entire nation "Bharata" and also to many parts of the Asian continent. But maybe it became difficult for the human race to accept and follow his path. That's why the existence of jealousy and violence continues on this planet.

These selfish worldly people couldn't accept Buddha's righteous paths. That is the human's unfortunate fate. People started treating Buddha, like God but were entirely unable to understand and follow his preachings. Very few people might have accepted his path to lead a peaceful desire-free life amongst the crores. Thus, desire kept on existing on this planet as part and parcel of this existence. Man could not free himself from the mundane thirst and longings. Everyone remained drowned in the ocean of their whims and fancies.

The world continued to remain the same with life going on the same way without any noticeable change. The way man lived before Buddha continued even after Buddha. Where is the change? Where is the purity? Though civilisation is progressing, awareness is increasing, but it is directionless. The right direction could not be given, to Buddha's divine realisation about the truth of life. Humans always kept themselves immersed in this ordinary life with materialistic thoughts instead of making an effort to attain "Nirvana".

So, it seems mortals have drifted far away from the teachings of Buddha. The distance is just immeasurable. Buddha's soul was crying for the lack of brotherhood within humanity and not fatherhood of the Almighty. Yet, humans couldn't bring themselves to believe in their brotherhood. As a result, various religions have cropped up focused on the fatherhood of the Almighty, spreading difference, hatred, violence and war in every corner of this globe.

Thus, in front of humanity, Buddha's teachings are crucified, making him a defeated Divine. Samay let out a long sigh and remained silent.

We finally reached the river bank where the boat was waiting for us. Sarnath, Uruvela, Niranjana everything slowly disappeared and became invisible. But Buddha's mystical form kept glowing within my soul.

As the boat kept sailing, a wave of thoughts flooded my mind, making me wonder about what I had just witnessed and what new realms of history were awaiting us…..

www.ingramcontent.com/pod-product-compliance
Ingram Content Group UK Ltd.
Pitfield, Milton Keynes, MK11 3LW, UK
UKHW021410190726
13845UKWH00028B/1009

9 789354 264740